TULSA CITY-COUNTY LIBRARY

D1175878

JUL - - 2022

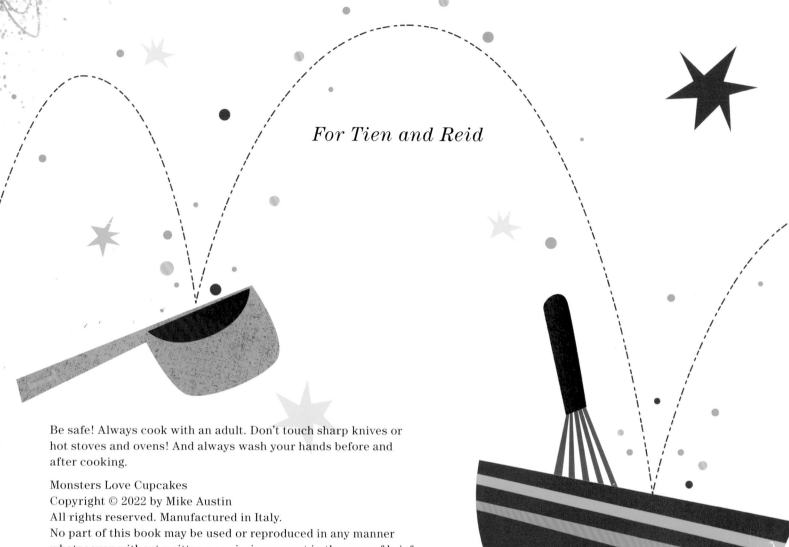

For Tien and Reid

Be safe! Always cook with an adult. Don't touch sharp knives or hot stoves and ovens! And always wash your hands before and after cooking.

Monsters Love Cupcakes
Copyright © 2022 by Mike Austin
All rights reserved. Manufactured in Italy.
No part of this book may be used or reproduced in any manner whatsoever without written permission except in the case of brief quotations embodied in critical articles and reviews. For information address HarperCollins Children's Books, a division of HarperCollins Publishers, 195 Broadway, New York, NY 10007.
 www.harpercollinschildrens.com

ISBN 978-0-06-228619-2

The artist used his favorite monster pencils, monster crayons, monster ink and brushes, a scanner, and Adobe Photoshop to create the digital illustrations for this book.
Typography by Mike Austin
22 23 24 25 26   RTLO   10 9 8 7 6 5 4 3 2 1
❖
First Edition

MONSTERS LOVE CUPCAKES

Written and illustrated by
Mike Austin

HARPER

An Imprint of HarperCollinsPublishers

Wake up.
Wake up.

Get out of bed!

Your extra special
day's ahead!

All your monster
friends are here

to celebrate this time of year!

Monsters measure.

One.

Two.

Three.

Monsters read the recipe.

A spoonful of

POP!

WOW!

POP!

POP!

A pinch of
FUN!

Monsters DANCE
and monsters

SING!

Monsters mix up
EVERYTHING!

Monsters **PLOP!**

PLOP!

PLOP!

PLOP!

And monsters

BAKE!

Monsters peek.

Monsters wai

And wait . . .

and wait .

and wait!

Smells so great!

Put them

on a plate

Now it's time to

DECORATE!

Monster icing.

Monster hugs.

LOVE

Monster kisses.

CHOCOLATE ANTS in UNDERPANTS!

YAY!
UNDERPANTS!
YIPPEE!

Monster BUGS!

All done.

So FUN!

Monsters share with everyone!

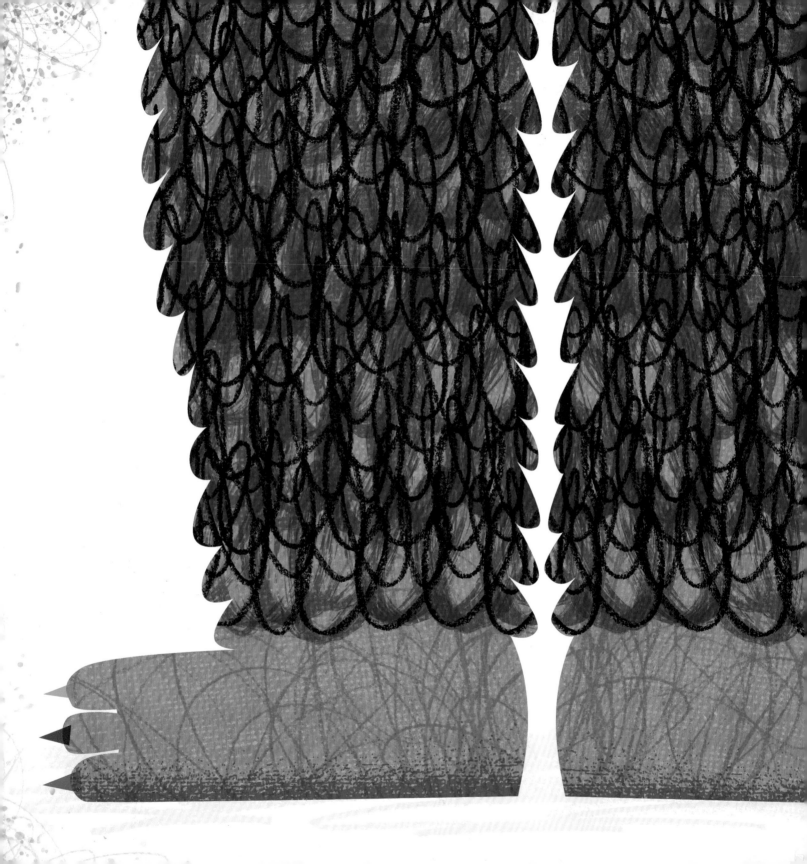

One
for big.

One
for small.

This one wants to eat them all!

HELP!

NOT SO
FAST,
BUSTER!

Make a wish.

For you
and me.

Best friends
we will always be.

Now it's time to

PAAA

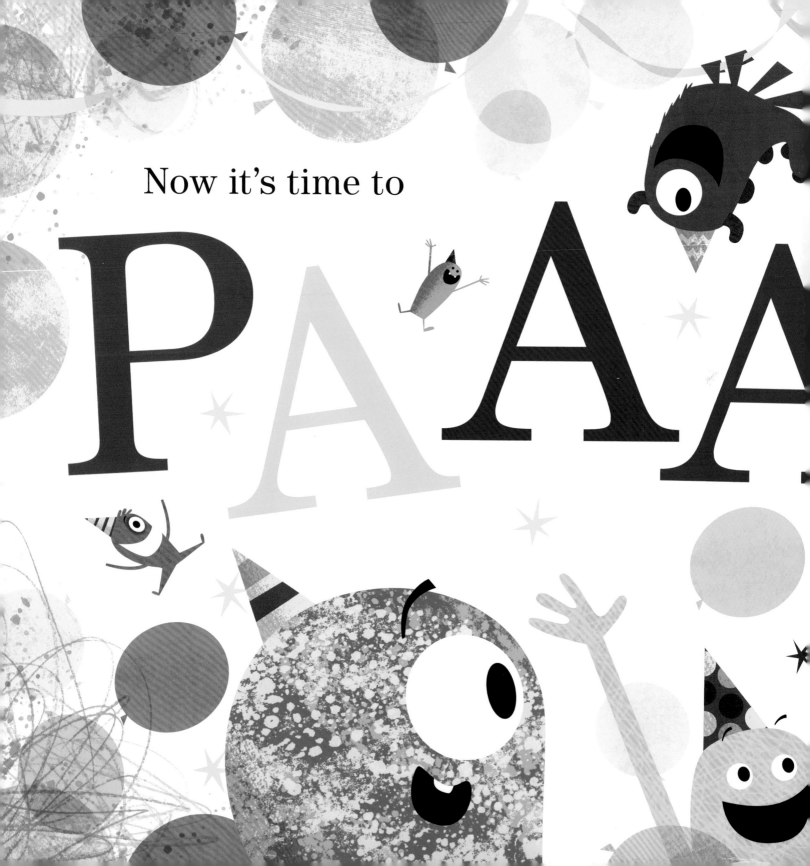

Green, red, yellow, brown.

WOOHOO!

PARTY

Monsters dancing all around!

It's your Happy

CUPCAKE Day!

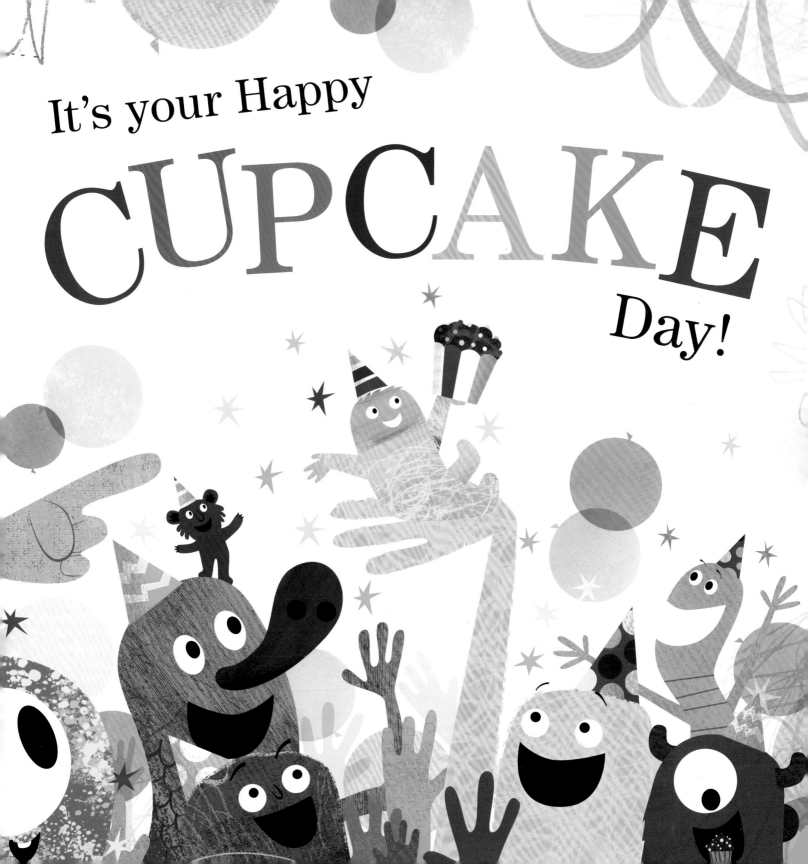